A Family Looks Like
LOVE

Written by
KAITLYN WELLS

Illustrated by
SAWYER CLOUD

FLAMINGO BOOKS

All puppies are born adorable, but they're not always the same. Some are big, some are little. Some are blue and others are speckled. They might have long legs, or stubby legs, or other times just three.

But usually puppies in the same family look rather alike. They have matching tails, or white paws like socks, or the same pointy ears that sometimes flip-flop.

One family knew this to be true because they had two similar dogs of their own. One was yellow like the sun, and the other was a beautiful brown, although from their curly tails to their scruffy coats they were the same.

The dogs had four puppies. The first three puppies
had scruffy yellow coats and pointy brown ears.
And they wobbled about on their short, stout legs.

But when the fourth puppy popped out,
she looked nothing like her siblings.

"This puppy looks completely different!"
everyone woofed.

WOOF!

The puppy had soft, colorful fur, her legs were long like noodles, and her tail curved like a curly fry. The family named this puppy . . .

Sutton Button.

One afternoon, Sutton and the pack went on their first outdoor adventure to the park.

Along the way, they met a great big dog with inky-black spots. Sutton was the only one who could reach the big dog's nose to greet him. "You're very lucky to be taller than your friends," the big dog said.

"Those aren't my friends. They're my siblings," Sutton replied.

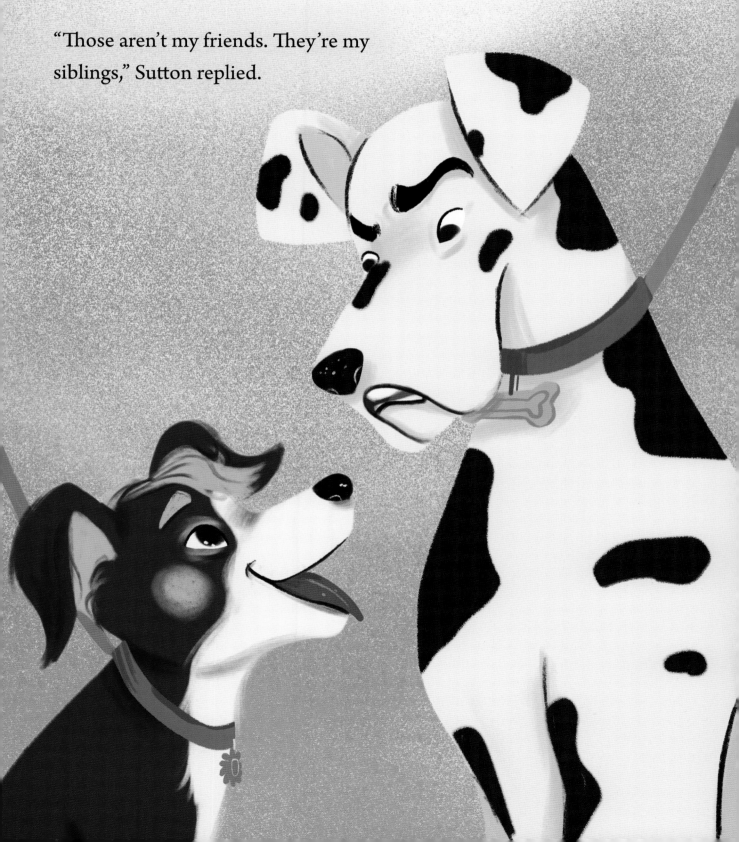

The big dog tilted his head in confusion. "That can't be so. Your legs are much too long," he said. "You look nothing alike."

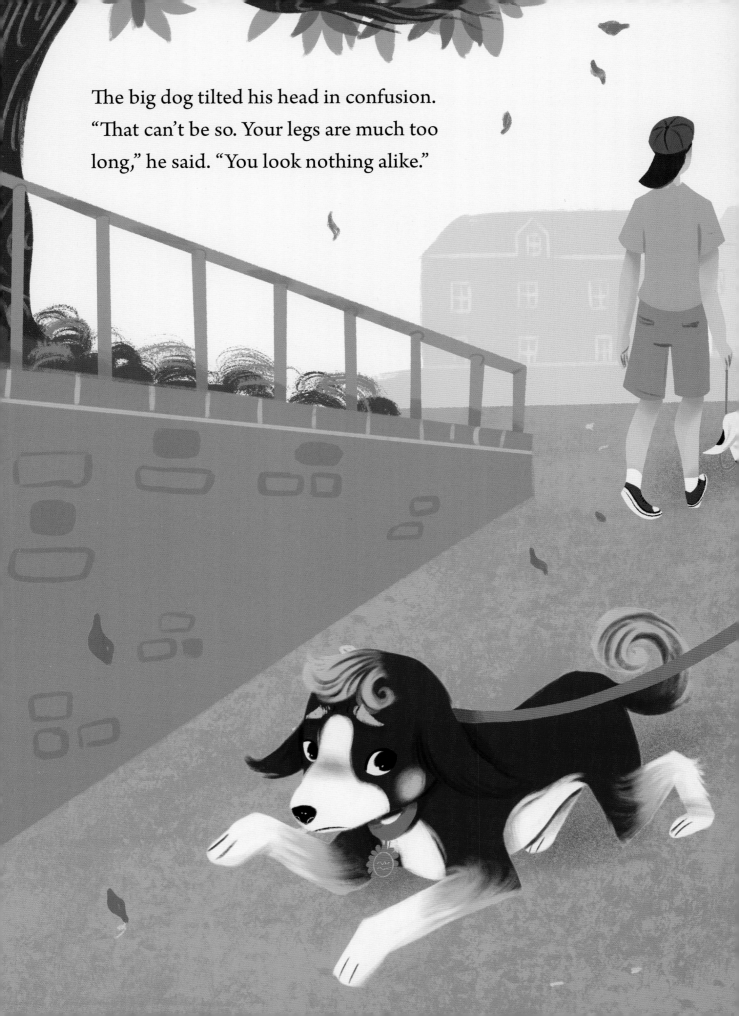

Sutton knew the big dog was right, and did her best to crouch down and be small as her siblings trotted by.

Soon it was playtime, and Sutton forgot all about the big dog's words. The puppies yelped and barked and growled and gruffed. They rolled in the grass and dug in the dirt!

Tired from all the fun, Sutton sat and listened to the birds chirp and the crickets sing.

A honeybee noticed Sutton sitting all alone beneath a flowering tree. "Why aren't you playing with your friendzz?" the bee buzzed.

"They aren't my friends, they're my siblings," Sutton said.

"I don't bee-lieve you," the bee zinged.
"Their fur is yellow, while you're mostly
brown." The bee buzzed back into their hive.

The honeybee's words stung,
but they gave Sutton an idea.

The little pup barked high above and asked the bee for some honey.

Then she rolled around in a pile of bright yellow pollen, making a sticky, sweet mess.

There! Now she looked like her siblings!

But not for long—

"Sutton Button, what happened?" her mom barked.
"Shouldn't you eat the honey, not play with it?"
her dad howled.

Before she could answer, Sutton's owners scooped her up for a much-needed bath. They washed away the honey and pollen until her beautiful mixed-brown fur appeared.

"I don't like the way I look," she whimpered.

Sutton told them all about what the big dog and the bee had said. "I don't look like I belong in our family."

"It's true," her mom said. "And that's okay."

Her dad nuzzled Sutton's forehead. "We may look different, but that doesn't mean we're not family."

"My coat is scruffy like your siblings'," Mom said. "Yet none of us like bath time."

"We both have legs that are good for running." Dad yawned as he stretched his long legs. "And you were brave enough to greet that big dog, just like your mama would have."

Her oldest brother piped up.
"We all have the same curly tails!"

"And we all love to roll in the grass
and dig in the dirt!" Sutton's
sister yelped.

"But most importantly," Mom
continued, "we all have big hearts.
You didn't get angry when the dog
and bee thought we weren't family,
and that can be hard to do."

"Not everyone will think we're a family," Dad said. "But all that matters is what we know in our hearts."

Sutton thought about what her family had said
as they went on their evening walk. She told
everyone she passed why they were a pack.

The big spotted dog heard about their matching tails.

The buzzing honeybee learned about their love of digging and running about. But the bee still didn't believe that they were related.

Sutton was hurt by the bee's brush-off.

Sutton thought back to her parents' words. "This is my family, believe it or not," she proudly told the bee. "And I don't need the same scruffy, bright yellow coat or short, stout legs to prove to you that I belong with them."

She pranced away, leaving the dazed bee behind.

The bee's words were soon forgotten as Sutton and her siblings rolled in the grass and dug in the dirt.

Sutton knew one thing for sure about her family: she loved every single one of them . . .

and they loved her, too.

DEAR READER,

Everyone has a special place in this world and we all deserve to be represented in the books we read. My own dog, Sutton, inspired me to write this book after I saw how well she gets along with everyone she meets. Like in the book, the real Sutton doesn't look like her puppy siblings, and she never thinks that any person or dog is better than anyone else. As for me, I grew up with a white mother and Black father in a place where not too many kids looked like me (not even my younger sister). I often felt like I didn't belong. The experiences Sutton has on her walk, when she's teased for looking different, happened to me growing up. While I didn't do anything as drastic as what Sutton does to fit in, I did feel quite mixed up about who I was meant to be.

I grew up in a home filled with love, and even though it was hard sometimes to look different, my family is what got me through it. You can be mixed, adopted, have two dads, or live with a grandparent—sometimes all of the above—but there is no wrong way for a family to look. There may be people who tell you otherwise, like strangers, your own relatives, or worse, yourself. But as long as you remember who you are and the people who love you, nothing else matters. Embrace what makes you different, and always pass along kindness to everyone you meet.

Puppy kisses,

Kaitlyn & Sutton

To my family, for teaching me to love myself —K. W.

To my peculiar family, I love you! —S. C.

FLAMINGO BOOKS
An imprint of Penguin Random House LLC, New York

First published in the United States of America by Flamingo Books,
an imprint of Penguin Random House LLC, 2022

Text copyright © 2022 by Kaitlyn Wells
Illustrations copyright © 2022 by Sawyer Cloud

Visit us online at penguinrandomhouse.com.

Library of Congress Cataloging-in-Publication Data is available.

Manufactured in China

ISBN 9780593403792

1 3 5 7 9 10 8 6 4 2

TOPL

Edited by Cheryl Eissing
Design by Monique Sterling
Text set in Arno Pro

Artwork created in Procreate on iPad Pro.

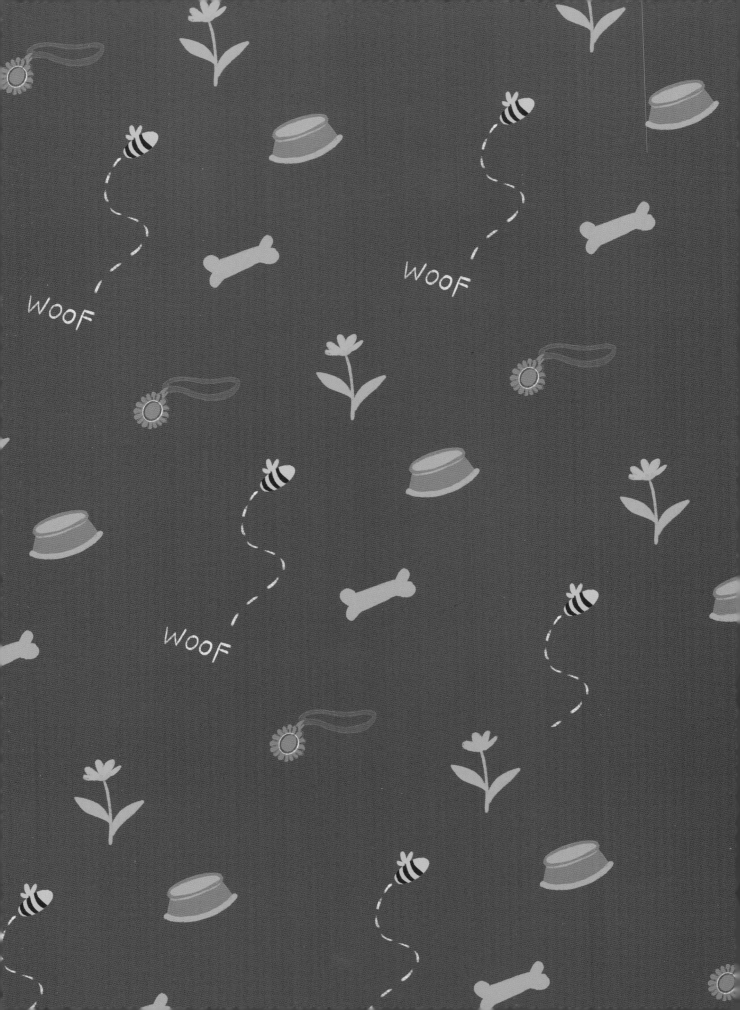